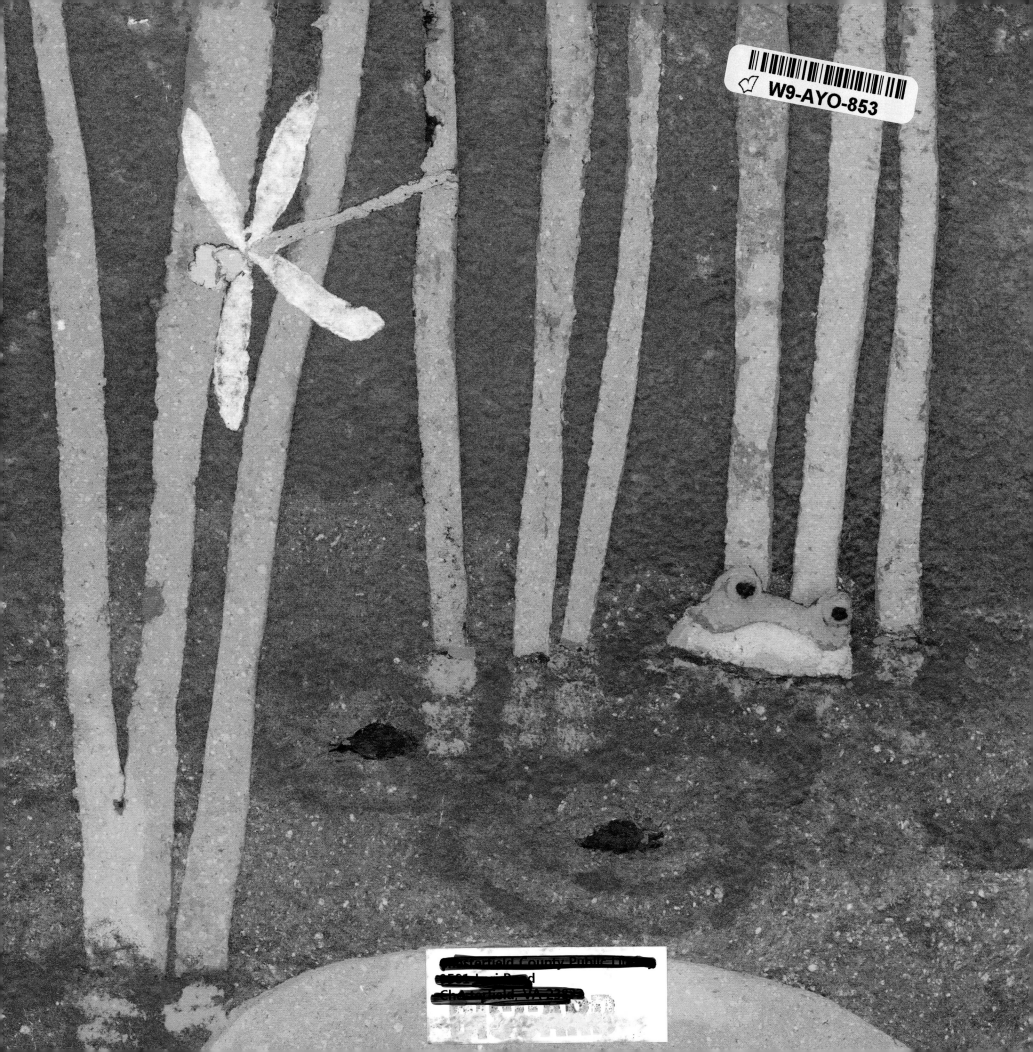

BEACH LANE BOOKS An imprint of Simon & Schuster Children's Publishing Division

1230 Avenue of the Americas, New York, New York 10020

BEACH LANE BOOKS is a trademark of Simon & Schuster, Inc.

For information about special discounts for bulk purchases, please contact Simon & Schuster
Special Sales at 1-866-506-1949 or business@simonandschuster.com.

The Simon & Schuster Speakers Bureau can bring authors to your live event.
For more information or to book an event, contact the Simon & Schuster Speakers Bureau at 1-866-248-3049 or visit our website at www.simonspeakers.com.

Book design by Denise Fleming and David Powers. The text for this book is set in Charcuterie Flared.

Manufactured in China. 0816 SCP

First Edition

2   4   6   8   10   9   7   5   3   1

Library of Congress Cataloging-in-Publication Data

Fleming, Denise, 1950– author, illustrator.

5 little ducks / Denise Fleming.—First edition.

pages cm

Summary: Each day, Papa Duck goes out with his ducklings but on Monday only four come back,
on Tuesday only three, but on Saturday all return when he calls and on Sunday, they stay home and rest.

ISBN 978-1-4814-2422-6 (hardcover)   ISBN 978-1-4814-2423-3 (eBook)

[1. Stories in rhyme. 2. Ducks—Fiction.] I. Title. II. Title: Five little ducks.

PZ8.3.F6378Aad 2015

[E]–dc23

2014042898

The illustrations were created by pulp painting—a paper-making technique using colored cotton fiber poured through hand-cut stencils.
Accents were added with pastel pencil. Visit DeniseFleming.com to see this unique process.

For my buddy,
Floyd Dickman

5 Little Ducks

Denise Fleming

BEACH LANE BOOKS · New York London Toronto Sydney New Delhi

5 little ducks went out Monday,

through the woods and far away.

Papa Duck called, "*Quack, quack, quack!*"
But only 4 little ducks came back.

4 little ducks went out Tuesday,
over the hills and far away.

Papa Duck called,
"*Quack, quack, quack!*"

But only **3** little ducks came back.

3 little ducks went out Wednesday,
past the paddock and far away.

Papa Duck called, *"Quack, quack, quack!"*
But only **2** little ducks came back.

2 little ducks went out Thursday,
across the fields and far away.

Papa Duck called, *"Quack, quack, quack!"*

But only **1** little duck came back.

1 little duck went out Friday,

down the road and far away.

Papa Duck called, *"Quack, quack, quack!"*

But **no** little ducks came back.

Papa Duck went out Saturday,
sad his little ducks were away.

So Papa Duck called,
"Quack, quack, quack!"

And **all** his little ducks came back!

5 little ducks woke up Sunday,
ready to leave the nest and play.

But Mama Duck said, "I know best—

today is the day we **all** rest!"

Mallard Duck Family
and Friends

Mallard Ducks

are wild dabbling ducks that dip their heads in the water and upend their tails to eat water plants. They also eat dragonflies, worms, beetles, and small fish. Male (boy) mallard ducks are called drakes. Drakes are known for their bright green heads. Female (girl) mallard ducks are called hens. Hens have a loud clear quack. Drakes have a raspy quiet quack.

Green Frogs

spend a great deal of time on the edge of freshwater ponds and lakes. They eat fish, snails, spiders, and insects. In winter, green frogs burrow into the mud at the bottom of the pond and sleep until it is spring.

Flying Squirrels

do not really fly—they glide. A soft furry membrane stretches from their front legs to their back legs and allows them to glide from tree to tree. Their tail works as a brake. These tiny animals make their homes in tree hollows and abandoned bird nests.

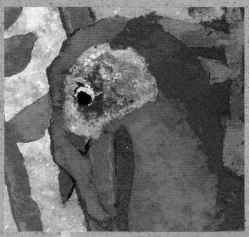

Wild Turkeys

live in forests and tall grasses. A male turkey is called a tom. Toms have very colorful feathers. Female turkeys are called hens. Hens have muted feathers. Wild turkeys make a gobbling sound. Even though turkeys are very big birds, they can fly for short distances. They roost in treetops and eat nuts, berries, and bugs.

Box Turtles

are land members of the pond turtle family. Their shell is domed and hinged at the bottom so it can be closed tightly for safety. Box turtles live an average of 50 years, but some live much longer. To survive winter they bury themselves in the ground. They eat bugs, slugs, earthworms, and fruit.

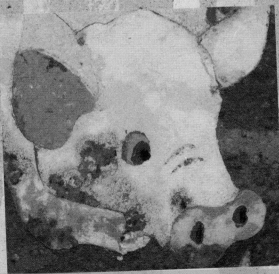

Pigs

have large heads and a long snout for digging in the dirt. They have four hoofed toes on each foot. Their feet are called trotters. Farm pigs eat corn and soybeans. Wild pigs eat plants and animals. Pigs are very smart, even smarter than dogs. A male pig is called a boar. A female pig is called a sow. Pigs are actually clean animals, but they roll in the mud to cool off.

squirrel photo bomb →

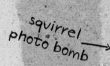

Anna

lives with her mom and dad in the yellow house. She loves animals, especially her dog, Patch. On hot days Anna plays in her wading pool. She has naturally curly hair, which she does not like to comb. She eats most everything. Her favorite food is pretzels.

On their daily walks the little ducks see lots of other creatures. Can you find dragonflies, whirligig beetles, flies, a rabbit, a deer, sheep, a horse, crows and other birds, a cat and her kittens, cows, squirrels, and a dog?